ANYA RICE AND THE TIME SLICE DEVICE

Contents

Chapter 1 Internet down!	7
Bonus: The Time-Travelling Cheese and Pickle Sandwich	20
Chapter 2 A girl called Noog	23
Bonus: How to speak Noog	36
Chapter 3 Parsnip Jack	39
Bonus: Bill's escape plan	54
Chapter 4 Mr Threadneedle	57
Bonus: Victorian school facts	70
Chapter 5 Air raid	73
Bonus: Threadneedle family tree	86
Chapter 6 Time spent well	89
Bonus: Time Slice Device timeline	104
About the author	106
About the illustrator	108
Book chat	110

CHAPTER 1

Internet down!

Anya Rice's time was precious. After a long week at school, Saturdays were for playing computer games, flopping in front of the TV or lying on her bed and watching videos on her phone. Her mum and dad often complained that she should be doing something more useful with her time, but that's just the sort of thing parents always say.

Then one lazy Saturday morning, the unthinkable happened.

"Mum! Nothing's working," yelled Anya. "The internet's gone down."

Anya's dad checked the router. "Yep, you're right, the light is orange. It's supposed to be blue. I'll call the help number."

There followed a series of long phone conversations, but with no success. Mr Rice sounded increasingly frustrated, while Anya's mood went from bad to worse.

"When I was your age, we didn't even have the internet," said her Mum, annoyingly. "We read books. We played with our friends. We found things to do. I remember, I could spend a whole day just with a cardboard box and my imagination."

Anya rolled her eyes. "It must have been very boring," she said.

"Actually no, I don't ever remember being bored … unlike you," said her mum.

"That's right," said her dad. "Your generation could do with being a bit more bored. Maybe we're better off without the internet … Oh, sorry. I wasn't talking to you," he said into the phone that he was still holding to his ear.

"What am I supposed to watch?" Anya flicked across the channels of daytime TV, with its endless supply of cooking shows, news programmes and soap operas. This was already proving to be the worst Saturday ever.

"You don't *have* to watch any TV," said her mum. "Why don't you read a book?"

She dropped one onto Anya's lap. It was a book an aunt had given her for Christmas, but which had sat gathering dust on her bedside table ever since.

Anya looked at the cover and read the title: *The Time-Travelling Cheese and Pickle Sandwich*. She sighed. She had never seen the point of reading stories about time travel. Everyone knew it was impossible to go back in time – and what was the point of reading about things that aren't possible?

"I'm going to the shops," said her mum. "Why don't you come with me?"

But Anya didn't want to go for a walk. She wanted the internet. She wanted her lazy Saturday morning. She wanted her precious time back.

Dad went upstairs, with tinny, on-hold music piping out of his phone.

Anya lay on the sofa, flicking through TV channels, muttering, "Boring … Boring … Boring."

The doorbell rang.

"Anya, will you get that?" yelled her dad, before adding into the phone, "No, sorry, not you."

Anya went to the door to find a postal worker holding a brown paper parcel in his hands. "Your neighbour isn't in. Could you sign for it and take it?"

"Which neighbour?"

"Er – " He looked at the name on the parcel. "Mr Butterwick."

Anya hesitated. Mr Butterwick was nice enough. Her parents said he was some kind of scientist, but she did sometimes hear strange noises coming from his garden. He had a tortoise called Keith. She had seen him having quite long conversations with it.

According to Archie Trencher, who lived on the other side of Mr Butterwick, their American neighbour worked for a secret organisation and was best avoided. Archie had told Anya about a time he agreed to water Mr Butterwick's plants and ended up on the other side of the universe!

"Is that OK?" asked the postal worker.

Thinking about it, Anya realised it was most likely Archie had made up that story. He had told her a few other unlikely stories. She signed for the package and took it into the kitchen. Apart from the address, there were no other markings on the package. She put it on the table, then went to look for something to eat.

The fridge offered very little of interest, so she closed the door again and turned around only to discover that the package was gone.

She looked around. Could it have fallen or slid off? It was nowhere. She looked inside drawers in case she had misremembered where she put it. She stepped out of the room, wondering if maybe her dad had come in and picked it up without her noticing, but she could hear his phone's on-hold music and her dad grumbling upstairs.

Anya turned around, looked at the table and saw that the package was back in the precise spot it was before, except it looked different now. The brown paper packaging had all but burnt away, its blackened edges smouldering. Anya could see a metal device inside. It was about the size of a toaster. Written on the side in large capital letters were the words: *Time Slice Device. CAUTION.*

Anya decided that she had better put the device somewhere safe in case it vanished again. She grabbed it and was carrying it to a cupboard when she heard a whirring and felt a light buzzing run through her fingers. Worrying she was about to be electrocuted, she tried to let go, but it was too late.

The kitchen flickered. At first, Anya thought it was the lights, but she quickly realised it was reality itself that was vanishing and reappearing. There was a sudden flash of light. The walls and ceiling fell away like a collapsing doll's house. The tiles dropped from beneath her feet. The world melted away and Anya fell.

Dropping down, Anya looked up and saw the sky flashing. When she finally landed, she felt damp ground underneath her and saw leafy trees looming over her head.

The world had returned, but it was no longer her world. The tree branches slowly parted and a pair of huge tusks appeared.

Anya looked up into the huge furry face of a woolly mammoth.

Now, Anya knew for a fact that mammoths had gone extinct, so it was surprising to be face to face with one. The mammoth tilted its enormous head, then snorted and jabbed a sharp tusk into her leg.

Anya quickly came to the conclusion that, under the circumstances, the best thing to do was … RUN!

When Sam and Ella eat one of Grandma's famous cheese and pickle sandwiches, they are suddenly transported back through time. Can they survive as gladiators? Can they outrun a T-Rex? Will they ever find their way back home? A rip-roaring, time-travelling, sandwich-munching adventure … funny and nail-bitingly exciting.

"Warning: may contain dinosaurs"
"A HISTORY sandwich with a MYSTERY filling! I loved it."
Ben Pulzeter, author of *Hogcart!*

"Wessord is a masterful story teller."
Nathan O'Jeerms, author of *Diary of a Dairy Cow*

CHAPTER 2
A girl called Noog

When she got up that morning, Anya had not expected to be transported back in time. She soon discovered that, while fluffy slippers and ketchup-stained pyjamas were perfect for lounging around the house, they were less well suited to being chased through a jungle by a woolly mammoth.

There wasn't a lot of time to think as she ran, but the thought did cross her mind that mammoths were vegetarian, so why was this one chasing her? Not that she could exactly stop, turn around and ask it: "Excuse me, Mammoth, why are you chasing me?"

She was also surprised to hear an almighty roar, until she realised the sound had not come from the mammoth, but from a sabre-toothed tiger. The mammoth ran in the opposite direction. The sabre-toothed tiger looked at Anya and licked its lips.

Anya understood that there was no way she could outrun this mighty hunter. It was only a matter of time now. *What a way to go*, she thought sadly. *Mauled by an animal that was extinct millions of years before I was even born.*

Just as it felt utterly hopeless, a hand reached out and grabbed her.

"Noog," said a voice.

Anya was dragged into the inside of a hollowed-out tree.

"Ow!" Her head banged against the rough bark.

"Noog," whispered the voice.

The sabre-toothed tiger scratched and growled, but the tree trunk was too narrow for it to get in. After a bit more frustrated chomping and growling, it gave up and slunk away, meaning Anya and the girl could crawl out of the tree trunk.

Anya did not want to let go of the Time Slice Device. She was desperately hoping it would fire up again and transport her back home. Her pyjama bottoms were soaked through. Her slippers were covered in what she hoped was mud, but rather suspected might be mammoth dung.

"Noog." Anya's rescuer was around her age. The cavegirl had long scraggly brown hair and wore a shawl made out of some kind of animal skin.

"Thank you," Anya panted.

"Noog," said the girl.

"Is that your name?" asked Anya. "I'm Anya."

"Noog … NOOG."

It wasn't much of a conversation.

"I'm from the future," she said pointlessly. "I've been transported back in time by this." She held up the Time Slice Device.

"Noog?"

The girl stared at her with fascination as she spoke, but showed no signs that she could understand a single word.

"It must be faulty. Hopefully it will take me back home – " Anya paused and considered this. "Except, I suppose, I won't actually be at home because I did all that running. Do you have to be in the exact spot to get transported directly back? I have no idea where I could be now. It looks very different."

She searched for a clue as to her whereabouts, but there were no streets, no houses, no signposts. There was nothing but dense green forest.

"Noog. Noog!" The girl scrambled up a tree trunk.

Even though she only knew one word, Anya felt sure the girl was warning her about something as she scurried up the tree. Maybe the sabre-toothed tiger was back. Or something equally scary. Anya grabbed the trunk and climbed, following the girl, with the Time Slice Device wedged under her arm.

"Noog." The girl reached out a hand to help her up.

Anya took her hand and started to climb, but then heard the whir and buzz of the Time Slice Device firing up again. It was about to transport her away.

"Nooog?" The cavegirl looked down at Anya in confusion.

"You need to let go now," said Anya. "Otherwise, you might end up jumping through time too."

The girl held on even tighter. "Nooooog," she said.

"Noog," said Anya. "Let me go."

The buzzing grew louder, and the world spiralled out of view, reminding Anya of water draining out of a bath. Before she knew it, Noog's grip was all she could feel. She was falling. Not from the tree, but through time itself. The flash of a million sunrises filled the sky and the world gushed back again.

Anya landed with a SPLAT!

For a moment, she was relieved that she had landed in something soft. Then, she realised it was something soft, wet and very smelly.

"Noooog." The girl held her nose and pulled a face.

"More like poo-g." Anya sat up.

"Noog?" Noog pointed up.

The sky had been blue before. Now it was grey.

The tree had vanished too. "Noog. Noog."

For some reason, the disappearance of the tree seemed to be the thing Noog was most alarmed about.

"It's probably been chopped down," said Anya. "Who knows when we are n-Ow!" Anya felt a sharp pain in her leg from a large metal fork being jabbed into it. On the other end of the fork, was a bearded man with frightened eyes and a scratchy sack tunic. He was jabbing the fork and muttering, "Witches. Witches!"

"Noog," said Noog.

"No," said Anya. "We're not witches. We're just in the wrong time."

"That's the sort of thing a witch would say," said the man.

"Listen, we'll probably vanish in a minute, so you really don't need to worry."

"Ha. You admitted you can turn invisible. If that isn't a confession, I don't know what is."

But Anya had suddenly realised there was nothing in her hands. "Er ... where is it?"

"What's wrong? Lost your wand, have you, witch?" said the man.

"My what? No, it's the Time Slice Device," said Anya.

She scrabbled to find it, feeling the squishy manure fill her fingernails, wondering if it was even possible for her day to get any worse.

"Witches!" yelled the man.

"Noog!" yelled Noog.

"Witches?" replied another.

"Noog."

"WITCHES!"

More villagers gathered, furiously brandishing their garden tools.

"We need a witch trial," said one.

"They've already confessed," replied the bearded man.

"Oh, that's helpful of them! Throw them up in the cage!"

"The cage!" cried the villagers. Rough hands dragged Anya and Noog out of the pile of manure and across a dirt path, before throwing them into a large wooden cage.

Yep, thought Anya, *it turns out this day could get worse.*

BONUS
How to speak Noog

Meaning: "Quick, get up this tree. The sabre-toothed tiger is back."

Meaning: "Hide in this tree trunk."

Meaning: "I don't understand what just happened."

Meaning: "Hello, my name is Noog. I'm very pleased to meet you."

CHAPTER 3

Parsnip Jack

Things were bad. Anya's slippers were now caked in mud, and worse, from two different eras. Her pyjamas were wet and filthy. She was locked in a large wooden cage and the Time Slice Device was lost in a large pile of manure. And now a mob of angry villagers had gathered around them to point and mutter amongst themselves.

As sorry as she felt for herself, Anya felt worse for Noog.

"Noog, Noog," she said, while clutching her legs and rocking back and forth.

"I did ask you to let go. If only you could understand."

"Your speech is strange," said a voice, "but I can understand you perfectly well."

Anya didn't notice the boy in the cage with them until he spoke.

"But I am struggling to understand your friend," he continued. "Is she from a foreign land?"

"No," said Anya. "Well, I suppose, yes in a way. Sort of."

The boy laughed and tapped his nose. "Ah, you'd rather not say. Good idea. As a fellow prisoner, I also keep my true identity hidden. In these parts, I am known only as Parsnip Jack." He then added with a whisper, "Although my name is actually Jack, but who would suspect that I would choose my own name? No one, that's who. Yes, you have to get up earlier than the birds to fool old Parsnip Jack."

Anya smiled. "Parsnip Jack?"

"Yes, I am the greatest parsnip thief in the whole of England … or at least from here to that big hill over there."

"Is a Parsnip Thief actually a thing?" said Anya.

"Of course," said the boy, proudly. "While others rob riches and gold, I deal only in parsnips."

"Wouldn't that mean you just end up with a load of parsnips?" asked Anya.

"Oh yes, far too many if I'm honest," replied Jack. "I've taken to giving them away, I have so many. I steal parsnips from those who have many and give them to those who have none."

"Oh, like Robin Hood?" said Anya.

"Who?"

"Robin Hood. From history," said Anya.

"What's history?" asked Jack.

"This is," replied Anya. "Except not for you, I suppose."

"It is hard to understand much of what you say. Are you really a witch?"

"No," said Anya.

"Really? Because you do look and act like one."

"I don't even have a pointy hat," said Anya. "I'm not a witch."

"Oh right, then I guess you'll drown when they dunk you."

"Dunk us?"

"Unless they decide to burn you," said Jack, cheerily.

"Noog?" said Noog.

"We need to get out." Anya rattled the door of the cage.

"Ah, well, luckily for you and your friend, I have a plan to get out of this cage."

"Noog?"

"Great. What is it?" asked Anya.

"What's what?" replied Jack, looking around.

"The plan."

"Ah, gather close and allow me to explain my plan." Jack leant forward, cupped his hand around his mouth and spoke in a whisper. "My plan is … we escape."

"Er, is that the whole plan?" asked Anya.

"It's more of an overview," admitted Jack. "Bill is the idea's man."

"Who's Bill?" asked Anya.

"He's second in command of my gang. It's just the two of us at the moment but we are looking to recruit. Say, how are you at stealing parsnips?"

"I've never tried."

"Yes, that's what Bill said when I first asked him. He's over there by the way." Jack pointed to a nearby pond.

"I can only see a duck," said Anya.

"Yes, that's Bill," said Jack. "Bill's my right-hand man."

"You mean, your right-hand duck," said Anya.

"They do say behind every truly great parsnip thief is an even greater duck," said Jack.

"Do they say that?" asked Anya.

"For sure they do. Hey, Bill, come and help us!" Jack waved at the duck, but it just quacked back at him and stayed where it was.

"Don't try and get that duck to help you again, Parsnip Jack," said a gruff-voiced villager. "Now you're friendly with witches, you'll be treated as one."

The angry mob were back. They opened the cage and hauled them all out.

"Witches! Let's dunk 'em then burn 'em!" yelled one.

"They won't burn if they've been dunked," said another.

"So we'll burn 'em then dunk 'em?"

"But then they'll be ash … and ash floats."

"Maybe we should dunk the duck."

"Nah. Duck's enjoy dunking. Dunking is water off a duck's back to a duck."

The villagers argued as they dragged Anya, Noog and Jack along the dirt path.

"Nooog, nooooog!" yelled Noog.

She grabbed Anya's hand. Anya saw she was pointing at a goat standing beside the path, nibbling a corner of the Time Slice Device.

"We need to grab it," yelled Anya.

"Grab what?" hollered Jack.

"That goat!" exclaimed Anya.

"Really?" said Jack. "Goats are all very well and good, but for a situation like this, you really do need a duck. I'll call Bill."

"Never mind your duck. We need the goat and we need it now."

Panic gripped Anya as she saw the goat step back, suddenly startled by the Time Slice Device. It was firing up again. Time was running out.

"Grab the goat, Jack!" she yelled.

"Oh, all right."

Jack kicked and thrashed, taking his captors by surprise. He wriggled free and slid across the mud, latching his hand onto the goat's leg.

"Noog, hang on!" yelled Anya.

With one hand, Anya held Jack. With the other, she had Noog, but the villagers held onto both Anya and Noog's ankles. If they didn't let go, they would all be transported through time.

An idea hit Anya. "You're right," she yelled. "We are witches. Hubble bubble and abracadabra."

"What are these strange words?" asked a terrified villager.

"They're spells of course. If you're not careful, I'll put a spell on you and turn you all into … er – "

"NOOG!"

"What's a Noog?" asked the villager.

"Oo, it's a terrible thing," said Anya.

The villagers let go of the suspected witches and were astonished to see them vanish into thin air.

"That was weird," said one of the villagers.

"That's magic, I guess," said another.

"Say, where's my goat gone?" said the third.

Bill's escape plan

The plan Bill the duck would have deployed had Jack had time to ask him.

DISTRACT
(Bill quacks loudly as a distraction.)

FLY
(Bill flies over the heads of the angry mob.)

BREAK LOCK
(Bill does this with his beak.)

ESCAPE
(Freed by Bill, our heroes are free to escape the cage.)

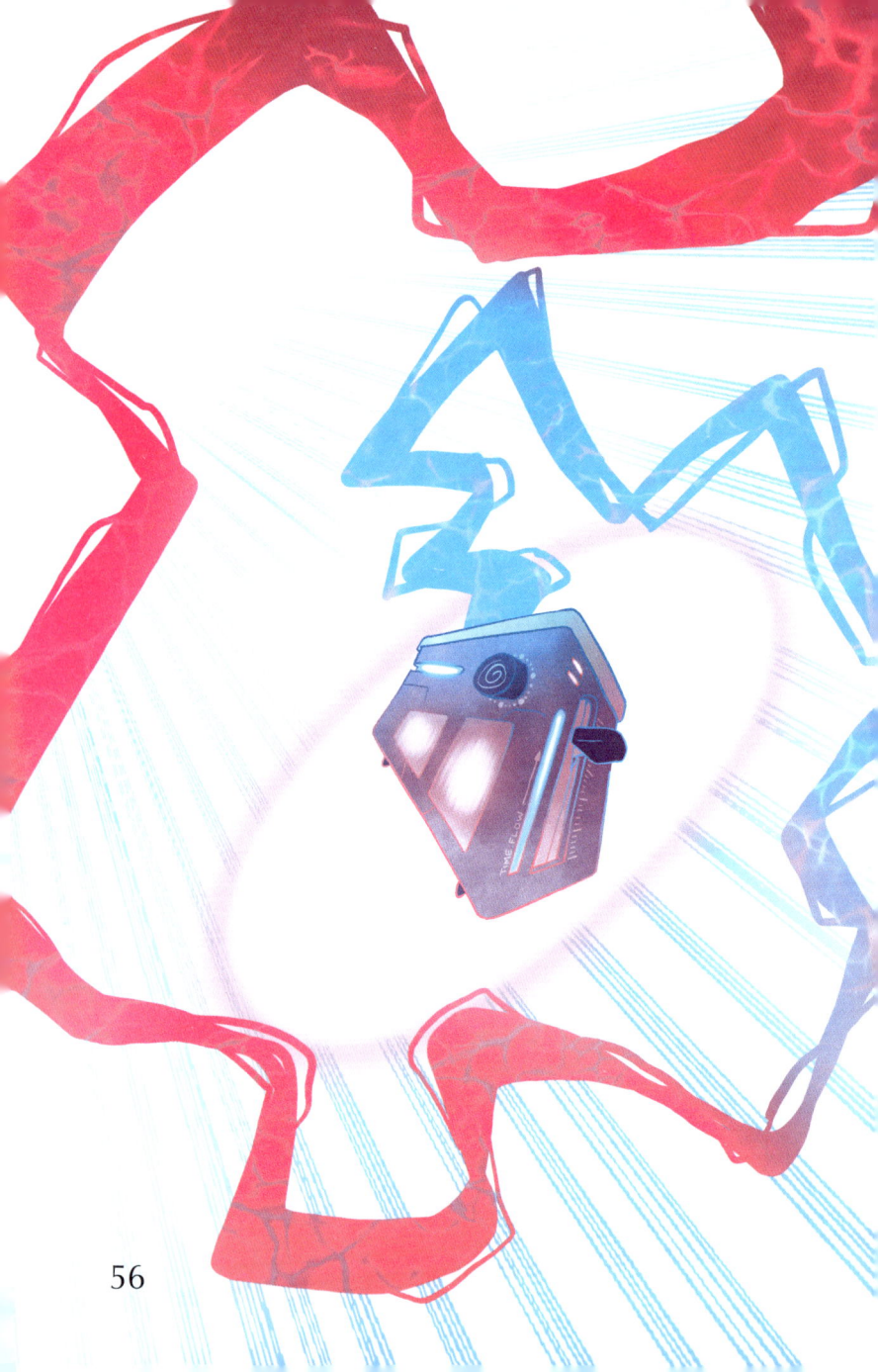

CHAPTER 4

Mr Threadneedle

Lights flashed and flickered as centuries whizzed by in seconds. As they slowed down, darkness fell. Anya looked up to see a building had appeared around them in the passing years. It took her a moment to realise it was a building she knew very well. She was in her school.

"Hey you, where did you appear from?" said a stern-faced gentleman at the front of the class.

Uniformed children behind desks turned around to stare at Anya.

"Eyes front, all of you." The teacher wore a black cape and hat. In his hand, he held a cane, which he brought down against his other palm.

"What's wrong? Cat got your tongue? And while you're explaining yourself, please also tell us about your friends, the medieval peasant, this cavegirl and … this goat?"

Anya turned around to see that Noog, Jack and the goat were all there too.

"Er, we are … we're putting on a play," said Anya.

"A play? What play? This is a school," said the teacher. "It is a place for education and for bettering oneself. It is a place to learn, recite and repeat. And then repeat. We do not … *play*."

"But it's a school play," said Anya.

"Never heard of such a thing. What are your names?"

"I'm Anya. This is Noog and Jack – "

"Parsnip Jack," said Jack.

"And the goat?" said Mr Threadneedle.

"I don't know the goat's name," said Anya.

"I think it's Judith," said Jack. "But it's not my goat and goats pretty much all look the same. Whereas, ducks – "

"Don't start on about ducks again," said Anya.

"I am Mr Threadneedle and this is my school. I have no idea how you have appeared in my classroom, but now you are here, you will do as you are told. Sit down all of you so I may continue the lesson. There are available desks for you all. Except for your goat. Animals are not permitted to sit at desks and have little need of Arithmetic."

"But – " Anya's words were cut off by Mr Threadneedle's threatening glare.

Anya gave up her protest and took a seat. The others did the same.

"Noog?" Noog picked up her piece of slate and sniffed the chalk.

"You use the chalk to write on it," whispered Anya, demonstrating.

"What strange land is this where children are taught such things?" asked Jack. "Is it a school for witches?"

"One more disruption and punishment will be swift," cried the teacher. "Now, write down the answers to these simple sums. Six multiplied by six."

Noog and Jack turned to look at Anya, both equally confused.

Anya didn't want to get told off again for talking, so she wrote down 36 on her board and held it up for them to see.

Both were doing their best to copy, when Mr Threadneedle stormed down the aisle towards them. "These constant interruptions are intolerable." He snatched the board out of Noog's hands. "Oh, 36. Very good, Miss Noog."

"Noog," said Noog.

"Wipe your slates clean and write down the answer to the sum, eight multiplied by seven."

Anya scribbled down 56, but the teacher was now watching Noog. He grabbed her slate again and held it up. "No, Miss Noog," he said. "The answer is *not* a crudely drawn mammoth."

The other children in the classroom giggled, sending Mr Threadneedle into a rage. "Be quiet, all of you!" he hollered. "The goat is the only one of you who is behaving."

The goat, who had been nibbling the edge of Anya's desk, looked up.

"Excuse me, could you tell me what year this is?" asked Anya.

"You don't know the year?" snapped Mr Threadneedle. "Honestly, what a sorry state of things. Even the youngest child in the school knows it is 1844 and our reigning monarch is – "

"Queen Victoria?" said Anya.

"Wow! How did you know that?" asked Jack.

"I told you. I'm from the future," she said.

"But isn't this the future?" said Jack.

"No, this is the past," said Anya. "Oh, except for you, I suppose it is the future."

"What nonsense," snapped Threadneedle. "This is the present."

"Noog."

"Why does she keep saying that?"

"I don't think they've invented language yet in her time," said Anya.

"You are all most peculiar," said Mr Threadneedle. "Not to mention, extremely disruptive."

"I'm sorry, but in a minute, we'll be on our way."

"Yes, we're witches, you see," said Jack.

"Witches?" repeated the schoolmaster. "You have no pointy hats."

"Jack, that's not helpful," Anya hissed, then turned back to Mr Threadneedle. "I'm sorry, Sir, but we're not witches. We are travelling through time and we're just waiting for this to go off so we can jump again." Anya held up the Time Slice Device.

"Give me that." Mr Threadneedle grabbed one end of it, but Anya was determined not to let it go this time. It was buzzing again.

"Noog, Jack, hold onto me," she said. "I think it's firing up."

"Noog?"

"Where will it take us next?" asked Jack. "This is actually quite fun."

"Fun?" said Anya. "This is a nightmare. We need to get to my time so I can find Mr Butterwick. He should be able to sort this all out and get you both back home."

"Who is this Mr Butterwick you speak of? Perhaps I should have a word with him." Mr Threadneedle was refusing to release the Time Slice Device.

"Oh, please let go," said Anya. "I don't want to take you as well."

"Take me where?"

Before Anya could reply, the goat suddenly jumped up and rammed its horns into Mr Threadneedle's bottom.

"Youch!" he cried.

But even a headbutt from a goat wouldn't make him release the Time Slice Device. The other children screamed in delight, then recoiled in horror as the time-travel machine transported Anya, Noog, Jack and Mr Threadneedle out of the room, leaving behind one rather confused-looking goat.

It was the fourth time Anya had time travelled that morning, but she hadn't got used to the unusual sensation yet. It was dizzying and confusing to see the time flying past, as though the world was being fast-forwarded. *Please let this be the last jump*, Anya thought. *Please let this one be home.*

BONUS

Victorian school facts

1844 was the year that Ragged Schools appeared in London. These were schools for poor children and named after the ragged clothes their pupils wore.

Class sizes were bigger in those days. One school in Hitchin had a classroom for 300 pupils!
Imagine that.

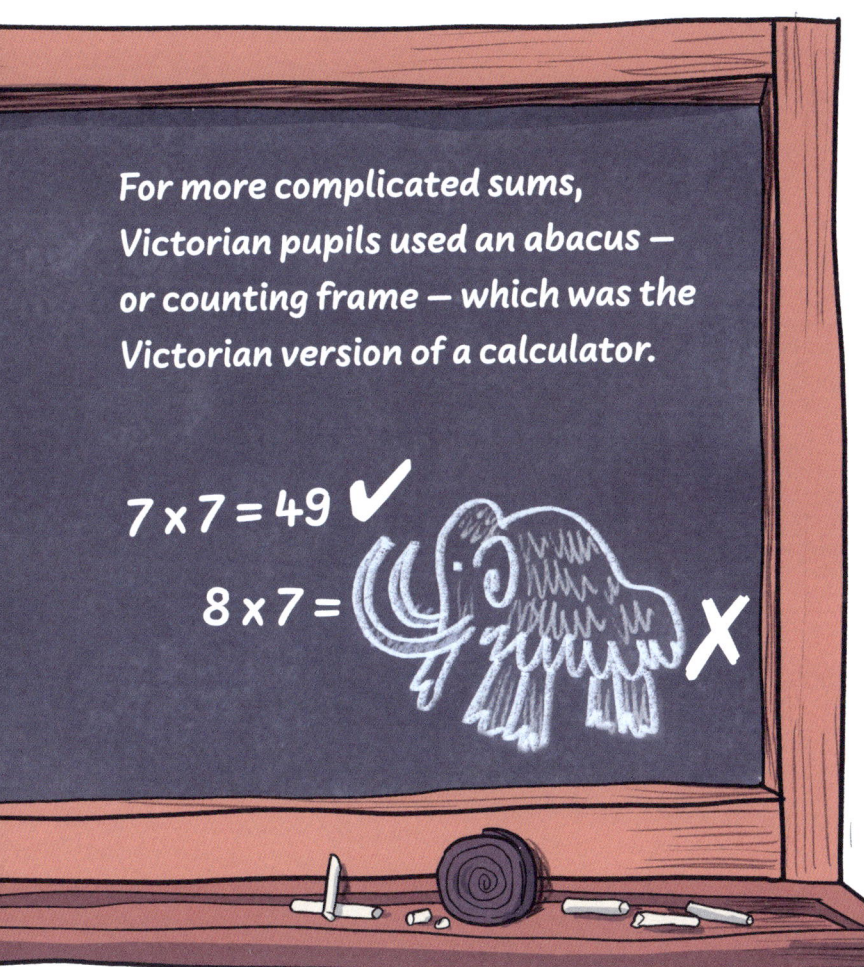

CHAPTER 5

Air raid

"What is going on?" Mr Threadneedle stood up and dusted himself down. "I say, why is it so dark?"

"I think it's night-time," said Jack.

"Night-time? But the school clock only just chimed noon." Mr Threadneedle pulled out a pocket watch, but it was too dark to read.

"Noog?" said Noog.

"Er, where is the rest of the class?" asked Mr Threadneedle.

"More to the point, where's Judith?" asked Jack.

"Judith?" said Mr Threadneedle.

"The goat."

"Never mind the goat. We've jumped again," said Anya. "But forwards or backwards?"

"What do you mean *jumped*?" demanded Mr Threadneedle.

Anya found a light switch.

Mr Threadneedle looked up at the bulb and took in his surroundings. It was the same school room, but now all the tables were pushed to the side and heavy curtains hung in front of the windows.

"Search for a clue about the date," said Anya.

"If someone doesn't explain what is happening, I shall – "

"I think I can explain. You are going to get us all killed," said a voice.

The light went off again.

"Hey," said Anya.

"Noog!"

"Oi, what's your game, lady?" Jack asked the owner of the voice.

"My game is safety. I am Winifred Bedford, and as the legal owner of this school, I must inform you that you are all trespassing."

"Madam, I – "

Winifred cut off Mr Threadneedle. "We are in the middle of an air raid and there is a blackout. If the bombers see this light, we'll all be done for."

"What's an air raid?" asked Jack.

"What's a blackout?" asked Mr Threadneedle.

"Noooog?" said Noog.

A siren sounded.

"Oh, I think I know. We did this last term. This is the Second World War" said Anya. "Which means that the year must be … er – " She tried desperately to remember what she had learnt when they did the topic in school.

"It is 1941, of course," said Winifred.

"Shouldn't we be sheltering underground?" asked Anya.

"Yes, we should. I was on my way when I saw this light come on. Please follow me."

"Madam, I will not take orders from you. I think you'll find these premises are under the name of Threadneedle."

"That is correct," replied Winfred.

"That is my name," said Mr Threadneedle.

"It is mine as well," she stated.

"I thought you said your surname was Bedford," said Anya.

"I married Thomas Bedford, although he is currently out of the country – " She broke off for a moment then continued. "Before I got married, my name was Winifred Threadneedle. This school has been in my family for generations."

"My name is Albert Threadneedle."

"That was my great-grandfather's name," said the woman. "It is a coincidence for sure, but one we should discuss once we are safely out of harm's way."

Anya had planned to spend the day with her toes pressed against a warm radiator, playing computer games and snacking. Instead, her pyjamas were caked in all sorts of disgusting stuff, her slippers were soaked, and she was huddled in a dark cellar with a bunch of people from all through time that she had only just met. She clutched her legs to keep warm and pushed her chin into her chest to try to stop her teeth from chattering. Her only hope was the Time Slice Device. She gripped it tightly. She was waiting for it to make a sound, but it had been hours now and the device had remained lifeless.

Anya wondered how many other people were also hiding underground. Some of the explosions were so close, they shook the foundations, sending clouds of dust from the ceiling.

"It should have come on again by now," she said. "We should have jumped."

"There is no jumping down here," said Winifred.

"I'm not supposed to be here," said Anya. "None of us should be here. Noog is supposed to be running around with mammoths. Jack is supposed to be stealing parsnips – "

"Ah, so you're one of those parsnip thieves, eh?" said Mr Threadneedle.

"Yes!" Jack turned to Anya. "You see, I told you it was a thing."

"It's not a thing," snapped Anya. "Mr Threadneedle is supposed to be shouting sums at children."

"And what about me, Anya?" said Winifred. "What am I *supposed* to be doing?"

"I er – "

"Am I *supposed* to endure this terrible war?"

"Er – "

"You say you're from the future. You think none of this matters, because it's already happened, but things don't only matter at the moment they happen."

"Yes, that's right," said Mr Threadneedle. "I always say that only through the study of history can we learn about our present."

"My father used to say something very similar," said Winifred.

"Your father?" said Mr Threadneedle. "I say, is it really possible that we are related? This is all so very strange."

"This is the worst Saturday ever," said Anya. "I'm so cold and miserable and I never asked to be here."

"Nor did any of us," said Winifred. "And yet here we are."

"It's not my fault," protested Anya. "But I'm tired and hungry. I'm both scared and bored, which I didn't even know was possible until now."

"Bored?" said Jack.

"Bored?" said Winifred and Mr Threadneedle.

"Noog?" said Noog.

"I don't mean bored. I just mean, well, you know. I'm uncomfortable and we've been here for hours. I just want to go home."

She was shaking the Time Slice Device in frustration, so it took her a moment to realise that it was vibrating again.

"Jack, Noog and Mr Threadneedle. Grab on."

"What about me?" said Winifred. "I think I like the sound of a future without bombs … without rations … without fear."

"Me too," said Jack.

"Noog-noog," Noog nodded.

"Yes, but this is your time," said Anya.

"I understand that very well, thank you," Winifred replied. "If you really are from a future in which this awful war has ended, then I hope that this experience will help you understand how lucky you are. I shall remain here and I will continue to appreciate every precious second of my life."

It was the last thing Anya heard before the vibration grew so large that the bomb shelter fell away and once again, the world glitched, then flickered away.

Threadneedle family tree

CHAPTER 6

Time spent well

"Where are we now?" asked Mr Threadneedle.

"I don't know," replied Anya. "Try to find a light switch."

"What's a light switch?" asked Jack.

"Noog."

Click.

When the light came on, Anya saw that it was Noog who had flicked the switch. She was looking very pleased with herself. They were still in the room under the school but now there were yellow safety notices on the wall and a stack of plastic chairs in one corner.

"Where's Winifred?" asked Mr Threadneedle.

"She must have chosen to stay," said Jack.

"An impressive woman," said Mr Threadneedle. "I think she was my great-granddaughter … Or she will be?"

Anya led the way up the stairs and pushed the door. She felt a moment of excitement as she recognised the artwork on the walls. She ran along the corridor to find a spot outside her classroom, and found a display about the Roman empire, including a drawing of a gladiator that she had been rather happy with when she drew it.

"I'm back," she said.

"Back where?" asked Jack.

Anya turned around and sighed. She was back in the right time, but Jack, Noog and Mr Threadneedle were still with her. This wasn't over yet.

"Come on," she said. "We'll have to go and find Mr Butterwick. He'll be able to get you all back home."

Mr Threadneedle was staring at a display about the Victorians. "I say, this is interesting. It says that Prince Albert will die in 1861."

"You probably shouldn't be reading that," said Anya.

"Noog?" Noog had found a display about how cave people made fire. She was rubbing her hands together, copying the picture.

"Come on, let's get out of here before this thing goes off again." Anya found a door and stepped out into the street.

She was relieved to see everything was back to normal, but for her companions, this was anything but normal and they all stared in wonder at this strange new world.

"What are these colourful metal carts that hurtle along the road?" asked Jack, standing far too close to the edge of the pavement for Anya's liking.

"They're called cars." Anya pulled him back. "And you do not want one to hit you."

"Noog!" Noog covered her ears with her palms as a large truck thundered past.

"What strange birds are they up in the sky?" demanded Mr Threadneedle, pointing up.

"They're called planes," said Anya.

"What are they for?" asked Mr Threadneedle.

"They have people inside," replied Anya.

"They must be very small people?" asked Jack.

"They're normal-sized people. The planes are just far away."

"Where are the people going that they should fly so high?" asked Mr Threadneedle. "To the moon?"

"No, probably on holiday. It doesn't matter. Listen, we just need to – "

"Anya?"

Anya turned to see her mother standing across the road from them, holding a bag of shopping.

"Er … Hi, Mum."

Anya's mum looked both ways and crossed the road towards her. "I thought you didn't want to leave the house today. Why are you wearing your pyjamas? Where have you been? You look like you've been rolling around in mud."

"Er, it's a long story," said Anya.

"Noog."

Anya's mum turned to look at the others. "Are these people with you, Anya?"

"I say, are those parsnips I spy?" asked Jack, peering into Mrs Rice's shopping bag.

"Keep your hands off that lady's vegetables, you no good parsnip thief," scolded Mr Threadneedle.

"It's still not a thing," said Anya.

"Who are they?" whispered her mother.

"Mr Threadneedle at your service, madam. I teach at the local school."

"Noog," said Noog.

Anya was relieved to hear her mum's phone bleep, but Jack, Noog and Mr Threadneedle recoiled and stared in astonishment as Mrs Rice pulled it from her pocket.

"It's a message from Dad. The internet is back up and running," she announced.

"In-turn-net," repeated Jack.

"You received a message? In your pocket?" asked Mr Threadneedle.

"Noog?" said Noog.

"Come on," said Anya. "Let's get you lot back to your own times."

As her mother was heading in the same direction, they all walked together.

"Please allow me to carry your heavy bag," said Mr Threadneedle.

"That's very kind of you, thank you," replied Anya's mum, handing the bag over to Mr Threadneedle. She didn't notice Jack reach in and snatch a parsnip.

Anya didn't enjoy the walk home at all, fearful of the Time Slice Device activating again. Her mum assumed Mr Threadneedle was her new teacher so kept quizzing him about how Anya was getting on at school. Anya supposed this was probably better than her talking to Jack or Noog, but even so, the walk seemed to last a very long time.

When they finally reached home, Mrs Rice relieved Mr Threadneedle of the shopping bag, and said, "Right, I'd better put this shopping away then. I suppose you'll want to get back to your room, Anya."

"Er, yes, maybe later," she replied.

Although she was keen to change her clothes, she was no longer excited about getting back to her lazy Saturday.

She needed to get this situation sorted! She headed straight back out, leading Noog, Jack and Mr Threadneedle across the front lawn. She knocked on Mr Butterwick's door and was relieved to find her neighbour was in.

Mr Butterwick opened the door and saw the Time Slice Device. He looked up at Anya and then Noog, Jack and Mr Threadneedle. "Oh dear, I was afraid something like this had happened. I'm sorry, er – "

"Anya," she said. "It's OK. It was actually kind of fun."

"Anya … Fun," said Noog.

"Noog, you spoke," said Anya.

"Noog," replied Noog.

"So, you have enjoyed your adventure?" said Mr Butterwick.

"Actually, yes," replied Anya. "I had planned to just sit around doing nothing, but if I'd done that, the day would have been over in a second. As it is, it feels like today has lasted much longer."

"Ha. As Bill says," said Jack. "Time spent well is worth more than all the parsnips in the world."

Anya doubted that anyone had ever said such a thing, least of all a medieval duck, but in that moment, she agreed with her friend's words.

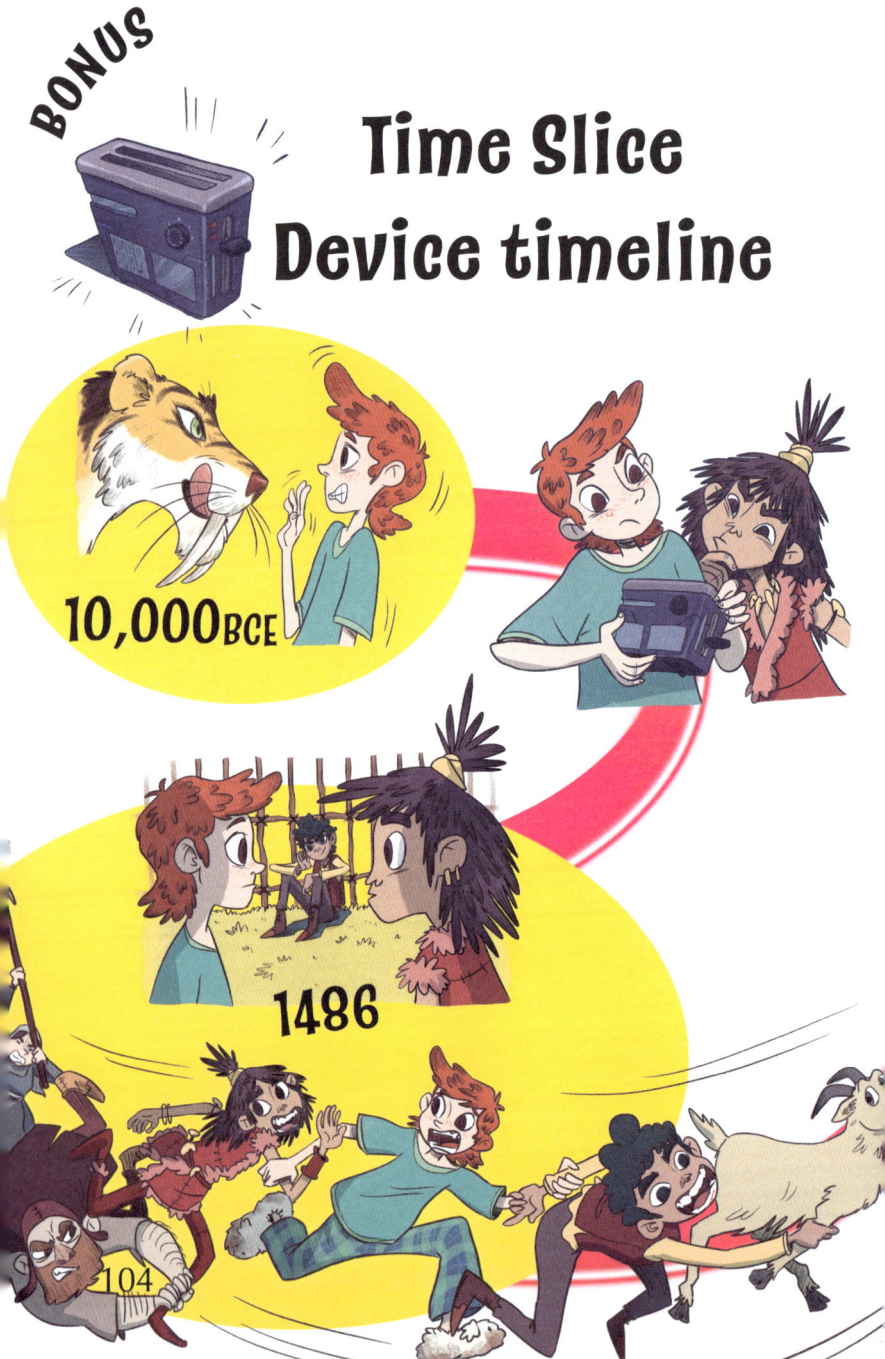

About the author

What made you think of this story?

I've written a few time-travel stories over the years and sometimes I get bogged down in the topsy-turvy timey-wimey stuff. With this one, I wanted to write a more straight-forward time-travel adventure, where I could just enjoy hopping across times zones.

Gareth P Jones

What does Anya learn?

I have noticed that when I have a busy day, doing lots of different things, it feels like there is more time in the day than those days when I'm sitting around doing nothing. Anya has to travel through time to learn this lesson, but for the rest of us, we can all find more time by making the most of every minute.

How do you come up with your characters?

I very rarely imagine what characters look like, and I often change their names as I go along, but I know I have a good character when I can hear their voice. Even with Noog (who only has one word) I very quickly got a sense of what she was like - and what she was trying to say.

How do you know if a book is going to be good or not?
I don't, but I did enjoy writing this one and I think there's a good chance that if you enjoy writing a book, readers will enjoy reading it.

Do you have a favourite character in this book?
Parsnip Jack made me laugh. I also like Winifred, even though her appearance is very brief, but I think my favourite is Noog, because I had to imagine what she was thinking every time she said, "Noog."

How did you choose the time periods that Anya visits?
Anya travels to four different time periods. I'm working on another book about cave people, so I made that the first stop. I've been reading a book about witch trials, so I made the second a medieval time period, when people were very scared about witches. While writing this story, I spent a lot of time travelling around London on buses and trains, where I am surrounded by lots of Victorian and Second World War history - which is why I chose those for Anya's final jumps.

Do you have a favourite part of the book and favourite illustration?
I love all the illustrations, so it's hard to pick, but I think my favourite is in Chapter 6 where they are all marching down the street with Anya's mum and Jack looks so delighted with his parsnip.

About the illustrator

Did you always want to be an illustrator?
Yes, ever since I was a child I dreamed of becoming an illustrator and comic artist.

Amerigo Pinelli

How did you get into illustrating?
I went to the art school of Naples in Italy and then to the comics school where I studied comics and illustration. But I had to wait some years doing different kinds of jobs around art and illustration until I had my first job as an illustrator. From that moment I started my career as a freelance artist.

Do you use pens and paints or do you work digitally?
More recently, I've been working digitally for all my jobs – I can't remember the last time I didn't. But I still love working with traditional tools if I can find time.

What was the most challenging thing about illustrating this book?
Making the characters move to several different historical ages in the same project was quite difficult. There was a lot to do to create an authentic atmosphere in each era.

What was your favourite scene to illustrate?
My favourite scene is when the goat, Jack, Anya, Noog and the villagers are running in a long chain across the book! It was such fun to draw and I hope that comes across when you are looking at the scene.

Do you do lots of research for historical scenes?
Yes I do, I love looking for references and researching clothes, interiors of houses and streets so that I can understand the mood of the age. Hopefully, I have managed to capture the essence of each historical period.

Which character in the book did you identify with the most?
Jack, of course! I love drawing funny, off the wall characters. Jack is so out of place even when he is in his own timeline.

Which character was the most fun to draw?
I love Noog. Her astonishment at the world and everything about her in different historical periods is so funny – that made it easy to draw her.

If you had a time-travel device, what historical era would you like to visit?
I think that I would try a time-travelling journey to the year 1200. The art, the spirituality and the culture of that age are so incredible!

Book chat

Which of the characters is your favourite and why?

Would you like to time travel? Where (and when) would you go?

What was your favourite part of the book? Why?

Do any of the characters change as a result of their time-travel experience?

What's your favourite illustration in the book?

If you could ask the author one question, what would it be?

Who would you recommend this book to and why?

What do you think happens next in the book?

Book challenge:

Design your own time-travel device with labels and instructions on how to use it.

Published by Collins
An imprint of HarperCollins*Publishers*

The News Building
1 London Bridge Street
London
SE1 9GF
UK

Macken House
39/40 Mayor Street Upper
Dublin 1
D01 C9W8
Ireland

Text © Gareth P Jones 2025
Design and illustrations © HarperCollins*Publishers* Limited 2025

10 9 8 7 6 5 4 3 2 1

ISBN 978-0-00-876797-6

All rights reserved. No part of this publication may be reproduced, stored in a retrieval system, or transmitted in any form by any means, electronic, mechanical, photocopying, recording or otherwise, without the prior written permission of the Publisher or a licence permitting restricted copying in the United Kingdom issued by the Copyright Licensing Agency Ltd, 5th Floor, Shackleton House, 4 Battle Bridge Lane, London SE1 2HX.

Without limiting the exclusive rights of any author, contributor or the publisher of this publication, any unauthorised use of this publication to train generative artificial intelligence (AI) technologies is expressly prohibited. HarperCollins also exercise their rights under Article 4(3) of the Digital Single Market Directive 2019/790 and expressly reserve this publication from the text and data mining exception.

British Library Cataloguing-in-Publication Data
A catalogue record for this publication is available from the British Library.

Download the teaching notes and word cards to accompany this book at:
http://littlewandle.org.uk/signupfluency/

Get the latest Collins Big Cat news at
collins.co.uk/collinsbigcat

Author: Gareth P Jones
Illustrator: Amerigo Pinelli (Advocate Art)
Publisher: Laura White
Commissioning editor and
    product manager: Caroline Green
Series editor: Charlotte Raby
Development editor: Catherine Baker
Project manager: Emily Hooton
Copyeditor: Sally Byford
Proofreader: Catherine Dakin
Cover designer: Sarah Finan
Typesetter: 2Hoots Publishing Services Ltd
Production controller: Katharine Willard

Printed in the UK.

MIX
Paper | Supporting responsible forestry
FSC™ C007454

This book contains FSC™ certified paper and other controlled sources to ensure responsible forest management.

For more information visit: www.harpercollins.co.uk/green

Made with responsibly sourced paper and vegetable ink

Scan to see how we are reducing our environmental impact.